Mike and Invisible Monster

Simon Spotlight
New York London Toronto Sydney New Delhi

SIMON SPOTLIGHT

An imprint of Simon & Schuster Children's Publishing Division

1230 Avenue of the Americas, New York, New York 10020

© 2014 Hit (MTK) Limited. Mike the Knight™ and logo and Be a Knight, Do It Right!™ are trademarks of Hit (MTK) Limited.

SIMON SPOTLIGHT and colophon are registered trademarks of Simon & Schuster, Inc.

For information about special discounts for bulk purchases, please contact Simon & Schuster Special Sales at 1-866-506-1949 or business@simonandschuster.com.

Manufactured in the United States of America 0814 LAK

10 9 8 7 6 5 4 3 2

ISBN 978-1-4814-0371-9

ISBN 978-1-4814-0372-6 (eBook)

I sing a song of
Mike the Knight,
who does what's brave
and does what's right.
And all the people,
great and small,
they know Mike will
protect them all!

Knights must always be on guard. It's their job to protect the kingdom from danger! Mike the Knight wanted to be a real knight, so he did what real knights do: He patrolled the village with his horse, Galahad.

"Huzzah!" Mike said as Galahad galloped over the bridge at top speed.

"Whoa!" cried Evie. "You almost knocked me over!"

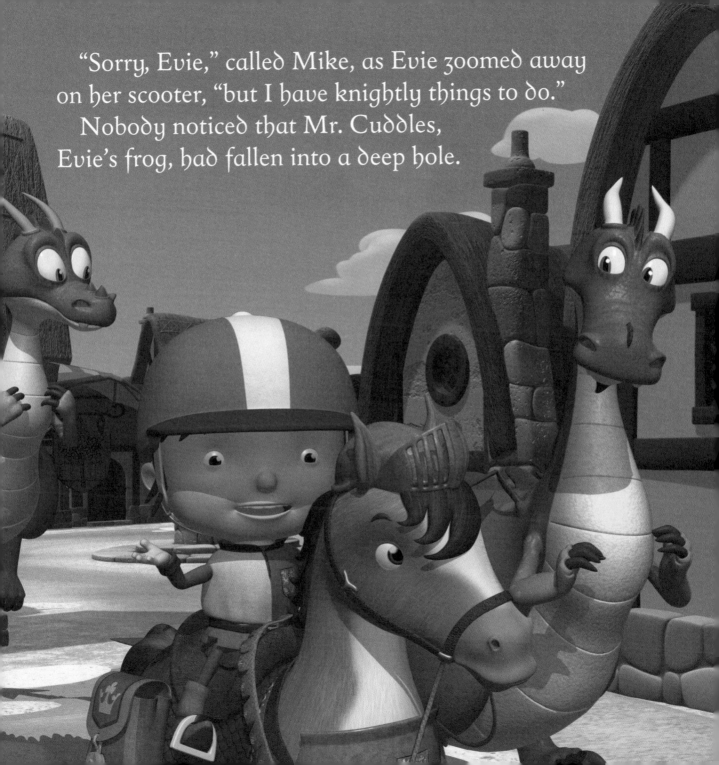

"Sorry, Evie," called Mike, as Evie zoomed away on her scooter, "but I have knightly things to do." Nobody noticed that Mr. Cuddles, Evie's frog, had fallen into a deep hole.

Suddenly, a roar came from under the bridge.
"GGrrrrr!"
Squirt trembled. "Ooh!" he said. "It sounds like there's a monster down there! I hope it doesn't attack the village."
They heard another roar!
"GGrrrrr!"

"By the king's crown, that's it! I'm Mike the Knight and my mission is to protect the villagers from the monster under the bridge!"

Mike raced back home, ran to his bedroom, and pulled the secret lever. Ready for action, Mike drew his enchanted sword. But instead of a sword, he had . . .

"A loaf of bread? How could that stop a monster?" he asked.

Mike and Galahad rushed into the courtyard. It was time to banish the monster from Glendragon and protect the villagers!

"Will you keep us safe?" asked Squirt. "I don't like monsters!"

"Of course," replied Mike. "I'm Mike the Knight. Onwards!"

"Woo-hoo!" cheered Sparkie.

"Huzzah!" shouted Mike as he raced back toward the village. But before he could start being brave, he needed to find some villagers to protect.

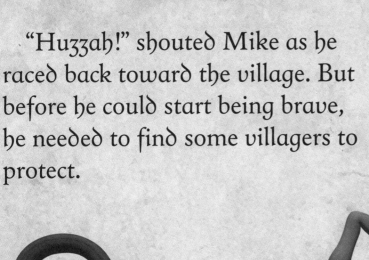

Then he saw a shepherd walking by.
"Aha!" cried Mike.

"Stay away from the bridge! There's a monster under it!" shouted Mike in a stern voice.

The shepherd frowned. He needed to take his sheep over the bridge and into the village.

"What kind of monster is it?" he asked Mike.

Just then, they heard a roar!

"GGrrrrr!"

"It's a Rotten Roaring Monster," announced Mike. "It wants to scare everyone!"

"We're lucky to have you here to protect us," said the shepherd.

Mike grinned at Galahad. The shepherd thought he was really brave!

Before Mike could get rid of the monster, he needed the right knightly tools. He asked Sparkie to go get his lance. Soon after Sparkie left, Mr. Blacksmith walked by.

"What's going on here?" asked Mr. Blacksmith. "I have to take this pile of wood to my workshop!"

Boom! Boom! Boom! The monster stomped up and down. Squirt shivered. "It sounds like it's got really big feet!"

"And lots of them," added Mike. "It must be a Hundred Hooved Monster!"

Soon, Sparkie returned with Mike's lance.

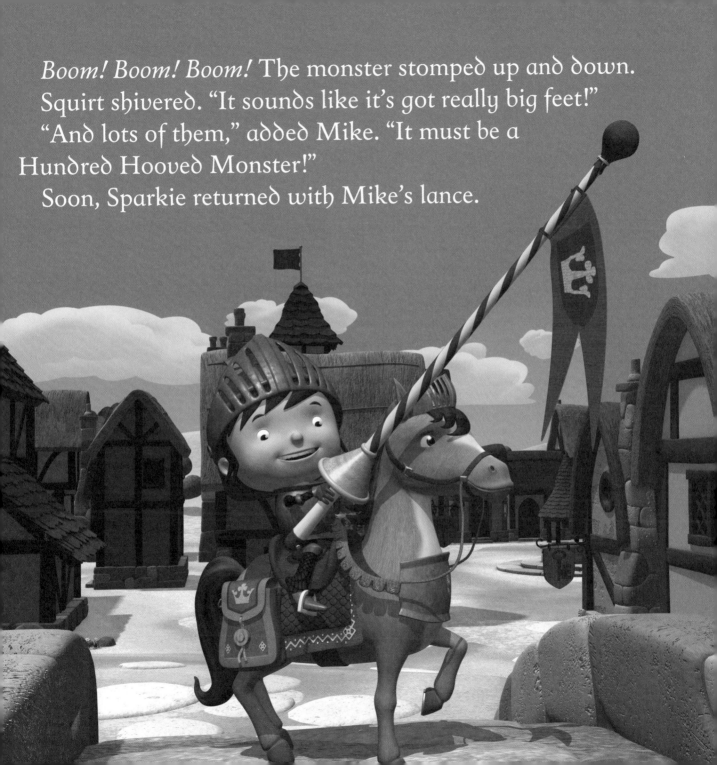

Even though Mike had his lance, he wasn't ready to deal with the monster. It was more fun being a hero! Instead, he asked Sparkie to go get his bow and arrows. That's when Mrs. Piecrust walked by.

"What's going on?" asked Mrs. Piecrust.

"There's a monster," explained Squirt.

Mrs. Piecrust looked puzzled. She needed to get to the bakery—she had pies in the oven!

Down in the hole, the monster's tummy started to rumble.
Ru-ru-ru-ru-rurr!
"He sounds hungry," warned Mike. "Like a Huge Hungry
Pie-Eating Monster!"

When Sparkie returned with Mike's bow and arrows, Mike showed off his archery skills to the villagers.

"Will you deal with the monster now, Mike?" asked Squirt.

Mike gulped. "Not yet. I need the . . . the catapult!"

The catapult was too heavy for Squirt to carry, so Sparkie got it and rolled it over to the bridge.

"There!" said Mrs. Piecrust. "Now you can catch that monster."

"I will," promised Mike. "I just need a . . ."

Suddenly, Evie appeared. "Help!" she sobbed. "I've lost Mr. Cuddles!"

"Evie!" shouted Mike. "Stay away from the bridge!"

"GGrrrrr!" came another growl.

"That sounded like Mr. Cuddles," gasped Evie. "I've got to save him!"

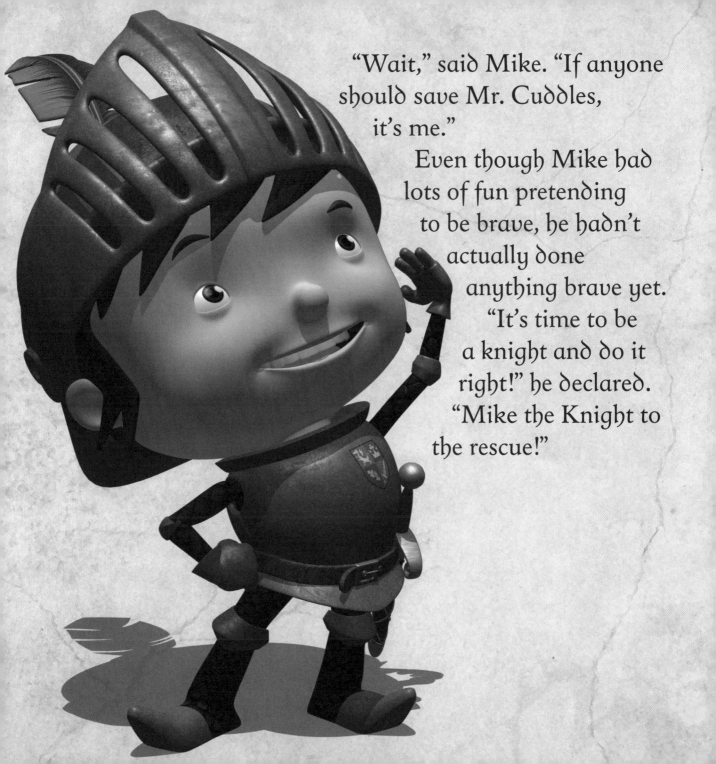

"Wait," said Mike. "If anyone should save Mr. Cuddles, it's me."

Even though Mike had lots of fun pretending to be brave, he hadn't actually done anything brave yet. "It's time to be a knight and do it right!" he declared. "Mike the Knight to the rescue!"

Mike drew his enchanted sword. Then he peered down the
hole. There, at the bottom, was Mr. Cuddles!

"Watch out for the monster!" called Mr. Blacksmith.

"It's Mr. Cuddles! But I can't reach him." Mike sighed.
"The hole is too deep."

Then Mike had an idea. He carefully lowered his bread sword into the hole.

"Easy does it," he whispered.

Mr. Cuddles bit into the bread. He ate his way from the bottom to the top of the baguette until . . . out he hopped!

"You saved Mr. Cuddles from the monster!" cheered Squirt. "You saved the village from the monster too!" added Sparkie.

"Actually," admitted Mike, "I don't think there ever was a monster."

Mike explained that the hole had made Mr. Cuddles's croaks sound louder and scarier, like monster growls.

"I'm sorry!" said Mike. "I guess I wasn't so brave after all."
Evie disagreed. "You were brave, Mike! You thought there
was a monster under the bridge and you tried to help."
Everyone cheered. "Huzzah!"